D0034380

Thiesing, Lisa.
The scarecrow's new
clothes : a silly thrill
c2006.
33305211430149
WO 10/30/06

A SILLY THRILLER WITH PEGGY THE PIG

LISA THIESING

DUTTON CHILDREN'S BOOKS • NEW YORK

For Jan, a real fashion plate
and storyteller extraordinaire

DUTTON CHILDREN'S BOOKS
A division of Penguin Young Readers Group

Published by the Penguin Group
Penguin Group (USA) Inc., 375 Hudson Street, New York, New York 10014, U.S.A.
Penguin Group (Canada), 90 Eglinton Avenue East, Suite 700, Toronto, Ontario, Canada M4P 2Y3,
(a division of Pearson Penguin Canada Inc.)
Penguin Books Ltd, 80 Strand, London WC2R 0RL, England
Penguin Ireland, 25 St Stephen's Green, Dublin 2, Ireland
(a division of Penguin Books Ltd)
Penguin Group (Australia), 250 Camberwell Road, Camberwell, Victoria 3124, Australia
(a division of Pearson Australia Group Pty Ltd)
Penguin Books India Pvt Ltd, 11 Community Centre, Panchsheel Park, New Delhi—110 017, India
Penguin Group (NZ), Cnr Airborne and Rosedale Roads, Albany, Auckland 1310, New Zealand
(a division of Pearson New Zealand Ltd)
Penguin Books (South Africa) (Pty) Ltd, 24 Sturdee Avenue, Rosebank, Johannesburg 2196, South Africa
Penguin Books Ltd, Registered Offices: 80 Strand, London WC2R 0RL, England

Copyright © 2006 by Lisa Thiesing
All rights reserved.

CIP Data is available.

Published in the United States by Dutton Children's Books,
a division of Penguin Young Readers Group
345 Hudson Street, New York, New York 10014
www.penguin.com/youngreaders

Designed by Jason Henry
Manufactured in China • First Edition
ISBN 0-525-47750-0
1 3 5 7 9 10 8 6 4 2

Peggy was a very snappy dresser.

She enjoyed having a different,

wonderful outfit for

each and every event.

It was five days before

the big party.

Peggy needed something

new to wear.

"I'm not going in this old dress!"

she snorted.

Peggy went into town to go shopping.

She went up one street and down another.

She searched high

and low in all the stores.

She tried on lots of clothes.

"I look ugly in this!"

Peggy said.

“I was hoping for beautiful,”

she muttered to herself.

But nothing was just right.

As Peggy walked home empty-handed,

she passed by a big cornfield.

From out of the corner of her little eye,

she spied something.

She walked over.

It was a scarecrow.

And it was wearing

the most wonderful outfit

she had ever seen!

Peggy was thrilled.

It looked just right.

But what to do?

"If I take it,

someone is sure to notice,"

she thought out loud.

Then she had a great idea.

Peggy ran home and

got some old clothes

out of her closet.

She thought that if

she traded one piece at a time,

no one would be any the wiser.

So each night,

Peggy snuck out into the field.

She swapped one piece of her old clothing

for one new piece of the scarecrow's.

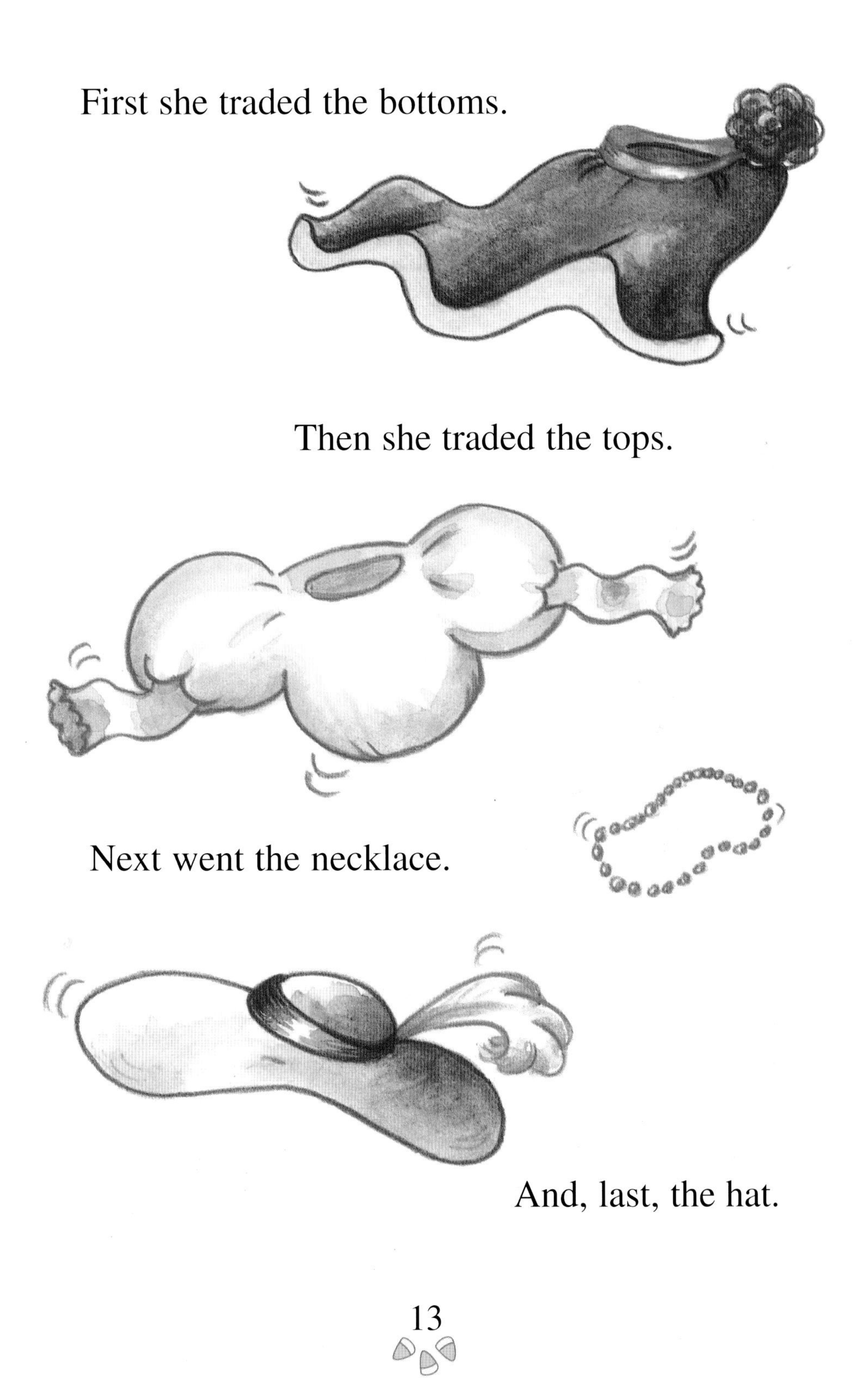

First she traded the bottoms.

Then she traded the tops.

Next went the necklace.

And, last, the hat.

At home,

she tried everything on.

"I love it!

I look fantastic!"

Peggy beamed.

She was so happy.

The scarecrow, however,

was not.

A scratchy voice was saying,

Give me back my clothes!

Give me back my clothes!

Give me back my clothes!

It got louder and louder.

Suddenly,

the door flew open.

Standing before her was the scarecrow!

"Give me back my clothes!"

the scarecrow yelled.

Peggy was so scared that

she could not say a word.

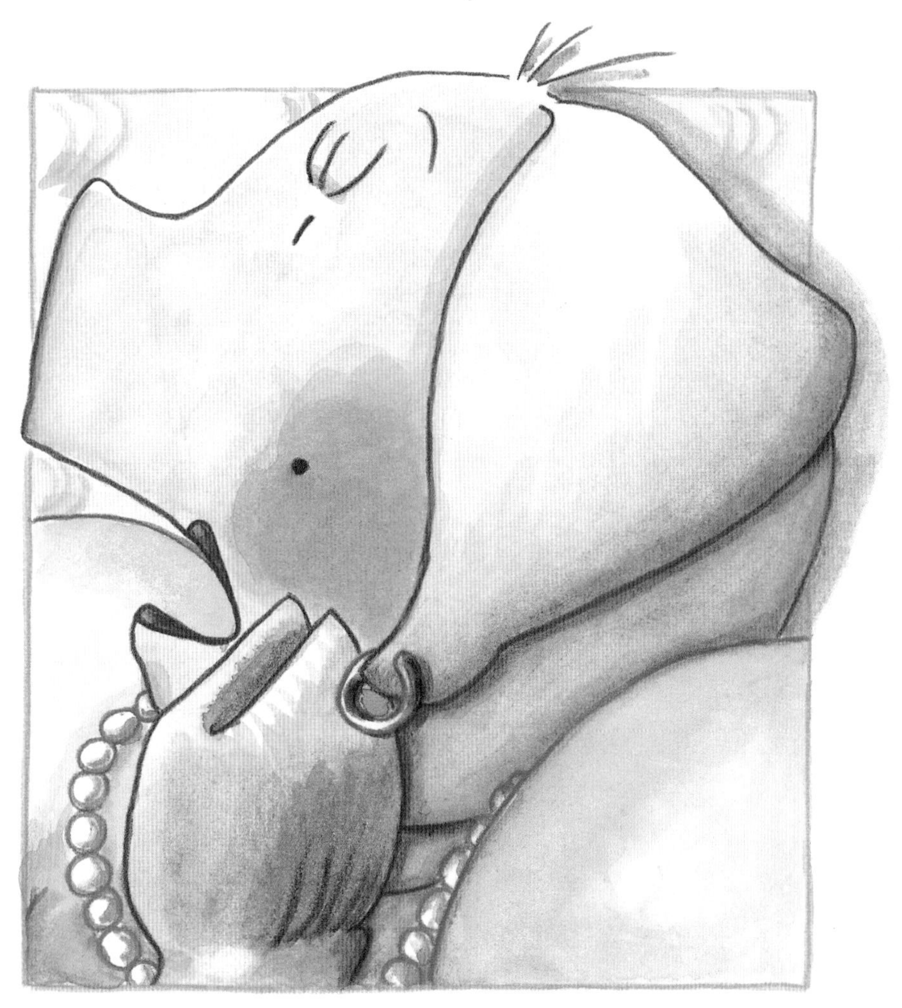

There was a zap of lightning,

a boom of thunder,

and out went the lights.

Give me back my clothes!

Peggy felt a cool breeze

against her warm skin.

Just like that,

the lights went on again.

And there was Peggy…

in her underpants!

"Oh my!" gasped Peggy.

"Hey! Give me back *my* clothes!"

she yelled.

But no one was there!

Then came a flash of lightning.

Peggy looked out her window.

She saw the scarecrow back in the field.

It was dressed in *her* perfect outfit!

Peggy put on her old clothes.

She felt like crying.

The storm passed.

Peggy left for the big party.

She was a little mad.

She had really wanted that new outfit.

As she walked by the field,

Peggy could hear the scarecrow,

laughing!

That made Peggy even madder.

She had had enough.

B

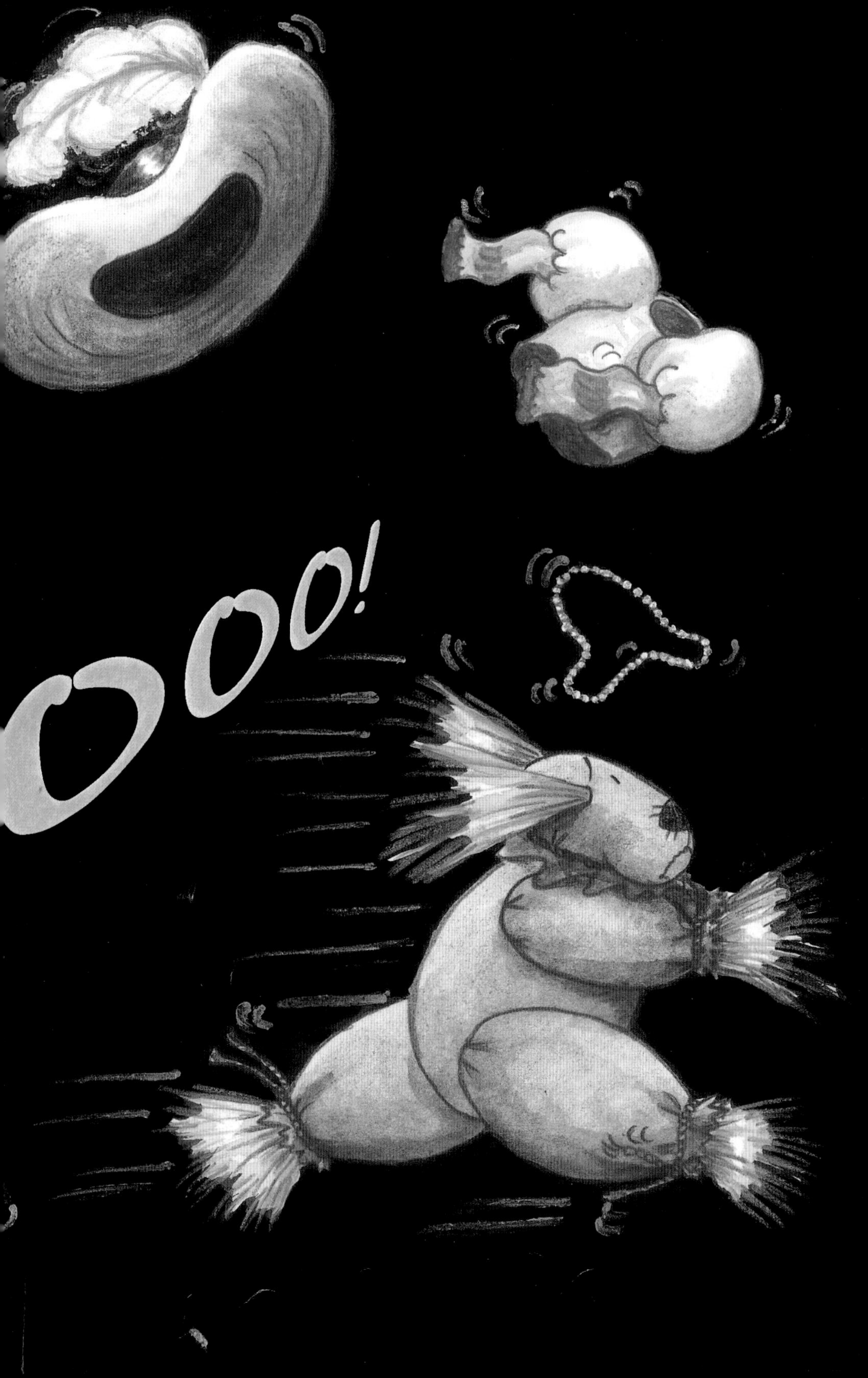
OOO!

Peggy put on

her new clothes.

And she never heard from

the scarecrow again.

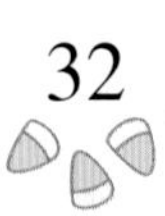